Mabel
One and Only

Margaret Muirhead

illustrated by
Lynne Avril

 Dial Books for Young Readers

For Abe, Zeke, and Pete –M.M.
To Lael and Darrell for their love and inspiration – L.A.

DIAL BOOKS FOR YOUNG READERS
A division of Penguin Young Readers Group
Published by The Penguin Group
Penguin Group (USA) Inc., 375 Hudson Street, New York, NY 10014, U.S.A.
Penguin Group (Canada), 90 Eglinton Avenue East, Suite 700, Toronto, Ontario, Canada M4P 2Y3 (a division of Pearson Penguin Canada Inc.) • Penguin Books Ltd, 80 Strand, London WC2R 0RL, England Penguin Ireland, 25 St. Stephen's Green, Dublin 2, Ireland (a division of Penguin Books Ltd) • Penguin Group (Australia), 250 Camberwell Road, Camberwell, Victoria 3124, Australia (a division of Pearson Australia Group Pty Ltd) • Penguin Books India Pvt Ltd, 11 Community Centre, Panchsheel Park, New Delhi - 110 017, India • Penguin Group (NZ), 67 Apollo Drive, Rosedale, North Shore 0632, New Zealand (a division of Pearson New Zealand Ltd) • Penguin Books (South Africa) (Pty) Ltd, 24 Sturdee Avenue, Rosebank, Johannesburg 2196, South Africa • Penguin Books Ltd, Registered Offices: 80 Strand, London WC2R 0RL, England

Text copyright © 2009 by Margaret Muirhead
Illustrations copyright © 2009 by Lynne Avril

Designed by Nancy R. Leo-Kelly
Text set in ITC Esprit
Manufactured in China on acid-free paper

1 3 5 7 9 10 8 6 4 2

Library of Congress Cataloging-in-Publication Data

Muirhead, Margaret.
Mabel, one and only / Margaret Muirhead ; illustrated by Lynne Avril.
p.   cm.
Summary: Mabel, who is the only child on her block, tries to find an adult to play with or help,
but all of her neighbors are busy and she and her dog Jack must make their own fun.
ISBN 978-0-8037-3198-1
[1. Play–Fiction. 2. Neighbors–Fiction. 3. Dogs–Fiction.] I. Avril, Lynne, date, ill. II. Title.
PZ7.M88465Mab 2009   [E]–dc22   2008001724

The art was created in gouache paint on gesso-covered bristol paper.

Mabel is the only kid on her block, unless you count Baby Walter down the street. But Mabel does *not* count Baby Walter because he can't do the things Mabel likes to do. Like go one-footed roller-skating or have a contest to see who can do the most cartwheels.

Grown-ups can do those things, but that doesn't mean they *will*. Luckily, there is Jack, who is Mabel's best friend and who can fit three tennis balls in his mouth at one time. But sometimes Mabel and Jack can't find anyone to play with.

"Shhh," says Mabel's dad. He is a
cartoonist and can draw any kind of
animal Mabel wants. But right now he
is looking at a blank piece of paper and
chewing on his pencil. "I'm trying to
think," he says.

So Mabel and Jack set off to visit Ms. Beadenbauble. Ms. Beadenbauble lives next door with Mr. Ernest Hemingway, who is the kind of dog that shivers and has to wear a sweater. "What a surprise," says Ms. Beadenbauble, opening her door.

DADS ROCK

"Greetings, earthling," says Mabel. "Can we come in and fish for coins?" Ms. Beadenbauble usually lets Mabel and Jack look under the sofa cushions for loose change. They have made a fortune this way. Mabel spends most of her quarters on tattoos or Super Balls.

"Sorry, dear," says Ms. Beadenbauble. "Mr. Ernest Hemingway and I are heading to the beauty shop to be shampooed and curled!" They zither off, in matching tennis sneakers.

Mabel and Jack hop over to Larry's. Larry lives in an apartment that smells warm and spicy like gingerbread, which makes sense because he's a baker. A baker *extraordinaire,* says Larry.

"Hi, Larry Extraordinary," says Mabel.

"It's the height of pie season, my sweets!" says Larry. His hair is white with flour and his shirt is covered in powdered handprints. "Peach peppermint strawberry coconut cream—I have so many orders, I can't keep them straight."

"We can help," says Mabel. Mabel is an expert taste-tester. "Just a morsel and a glass of milk will do."

"I'm too busy for taste-testing today, my muffins," says Larry. "I can't even find the table!"

Mabel and Jack scoot
on over to Mr. Woodrow's
garden. Mr. Woodrow
is there, surrounded by
sunflowers with giant
drooping faces.

"Need any digging?" Mabel asks. Jack is excellent at digging holes, except when he digs holes in the wrong places, like where Mr. Woodrow's prize roses used to be.

"Not today, folks," says Mr. Woodrow. "I've got a bug problem. If I don't do something soon, these critters will eat everything."

"I think one is eating your hat," says Mabel.

"So it is," says Mr. Woodrow.

Mabel and Jack say good-bye to Mr. Woodrow.
They find a sunny spot to sit. "I've got a grown-
up problem," Mabel says to Jack. "Grown-ups
are always trying to think or going to the beauty
shop or baking pies or fighting bugs." Mabel
feels lonely. Jack rests his chin on his paw. "Jack,
you're my best friend," says Mabel.

Mabel decides to stand on her hands. Upside-
down, the buildings on her block look like
ships floating in the sky, and the flowers in Mr.
Woodrow's garden dangle like yellow stars.

Mabel thinks up an idea. Then another idea, and another. "Upside-down is good for ideas," Mabel says to Jack.

First Mabel invents Super Ball bowling, which is a very good game until Jack almost swallows a Super Ball.

Then Mabel and Jack look for interesting trash.
They find three bottle caps, a bent bicycle wheel,
and a cardboard box.

They climb inside the box . . .

and fly to outer space.

An hour or two later, Mabel's dad peers into the space module. "Anyone for one-footed roller-skating?" he asks.

"Can't. I'm not even on this planet," says Mabel.

Her dad leaves and comes back with Mr. Woodrow. "Can I offer you a gift?" asks Mr. Woodrow, who is carrying a jar with a leaf and a bug inside.

"Nice specimen," Mabel says. "Just leave it with the space dog."

Next Mabel spies the splattered and sprinkled shoes of Larry Extraordinary. "I've brought cookies, my sugar dumplings," he says.

Mabel accepts the cookies, but she won't come out and no one is allowed in. "There isn't enough air in here," she says.

Suddenly a shampooed-and-curled Ms. Beadenbauble floats into view, next to a shampooed-and-curled Mr. Ernest Hemingway. "Please, please come back," Ms. Beadenbauble says. "We miss you terribly."

"I don't know," says Mabel. "I'm really awfully busy." She looks at the grown-up faces crowding the space window. They look as if they don't have any good ideas of their own.

"Okay," Mabel says finally, climbing out of her spaceship. After all, she *is* the only kid on the block (unless you count Baby Walter), and what would they ever do without her?

"Let's have a cartwheel contest!"